HEARTS TIGHTLY

KNIT

HEARTS
TIGHTLY KNIT

Twins & Needles Book 1

Anita,
Thank you for
your faithful
prayer support.
love,
Jodie Heb. 11:1

Jodie Wolfe

Copyright © 2016 Jodie Wolfe

jodiewolfe@comcast.net

Printed in the United States of America

Hearts Tightly Knit/ Jodie Wolfe
Trade Paperback ISBN: 978-0-9975026-0-2
ISBN: 0-9975026-0-6

Wolfe, Jodie:
    Hearts Tightly Knit: a novel/Jodie Wolfe
    (Twins & Needles; Book 1)
1.   History—Romance—Fiction.   2.   Christian—Inspirational—Fiction.   3. Texas—Western—Fiction. 4. History—The Children's Aid Society—Fiction. 5. Series—Twins & Needles. 6. Twins—Fiction.

All scripture is taken from the KJV of the Bible

First Edition

14 13 12 11 10 / 10 9 8 7 6 5 4 3 2 1

My first praise goes to my Lord and Savior, who instilled in me the love of story.

To my wonderful husband who supports, encourages, and prays for me daily. You are my best friend and cheerleader. Thank you for all you have done to help me along in this writing journey. I praise God for you!

Thank you to my faithful prayer partners.

Special thanks to Loni Myers and Lori Weibley for allowing me a glimpse into the world of twins.

Thank you to my fellow writers at Quid Pro Quills - for their keen eyes and helpful critiques.

To God be the glory.

Hide not thy face far from me; put not thy servant away in anger: thou hast been my help; leave me not, neither forsake me, O God of my salvation. When my father and my mother forsake me, then the LORD will take me up.
Psalm 27:9-10 (KJV)

Chapter One

Calder Springs, Texas 1875

"EllieMae, some fella's here to court you."
Mrs. Wright's words meandered up the steps,
along with the scent of fried chicken, to the
small bedroom.

Ellie Stafford flicked the lace curtain aside
and caught sight of a dusty horse tied to the
hitching post out front. She shook her head and
turned toward her sister. "Do you think our
landlady will ever be able to tell us apart?
We've been living in her boarding house for

years, and she still can't. What's this make now? The tenth man who has come calling?"

"Twelfth, I think. At least here in Texas." Mae, her identical twin, stood and eased the kinks from her back.

"That's not counting all the proposals on the Orphan Train from New York." Ellie sank into the straight-back chair in front of a worn dressing table. She took one last look at her reflection and tucked a brown wisp behind her ear.

"Heavens no. There were too many to keep a tally of them while we traveled. Besides, that was seven years ago." Mae smoothed the wrinkles from her pink chiffon gown. "I may have lost count after the banker knelt on one knee in the middle of the street and almost got ran over by a runaway wagon."

Ellie snorted. "I almost forgot about that one. He didn't care which of us said yes as long as one of us—"

"Accepted." Mae nodded. "Men. They should know by now we aren't interested."

"EllieMae!" Mrs. Wright's voice raised another octave.

Ellie sighed and clasped her sister's hand. "Well, I guess we better get to it then." They padded down the steps.

"Remember our promise," Mae whispered before they entered the sitting room.

As if she'd ever forget.

Mrs. Wright stood in the center of the room with her hands jammed onto her plump waist, her wrinkled face dripping with sweat.

Mae hugged the woman's shoulders and murmured something to her. Must mean it was Ellie's turn to get rid of the intruder while the other calmed their landlady.

A tall, broad-shouldered man filled the room and made it feel cramped. His hip rested against the upright piano. He turned from gazing out the window and studied them. He swept his Stetson off, almost as an afterthought. Blond curls tumbled onto his forehead. His bright blue eyes held Ellie's before flickering to her sister. Stubble dotted his handsome face.

"I'm sorry, but we aren't interested in marriage." Ellie pointed to the door. "Thank you for coming."

His eyebrows arched high as he glanced between the two of them again. "Never said nothing about marriage."

Mae sidled up beside her. "What do you want then?"

"A cook." His fingers curled around the brim of his hat.

Ellie's hand flew to her bosom. "You aren't here to propose to—"

"One of us?" Mae shot a quick look her way.

He rubbed the whiskers on his chin. "What kind of fool would want to do that?"

Mrs. Wright puffed as she edged closer to the stranger and poked him in the chest. "See here. I run a respectable boarding house. If you don't have anything nice to say to the ladies, then you best be on your way."

He held up his hands. "I didn't mean no harm."

Their landlady whipped off her apron and swung it in his direction. "Git, I say." She flicked it against his arm.

The cowboy didn't flinch. Not that a piece of fabric could do any damage, but the stocky woman widened the cloth as if she faced a bull. She alternated between snapping the fabric and jabbing her fingers into his muscled body until she corralled him in the direction of the front door.

"You git, and don't come back." Mrs. Wright took one more swing at the man.

Ellie refrained from joining the fracas. His piercing eyes held hers for a fraction of a second before he left. An odd sensation stirred through her body and made her arms tingle like a lightning storm was headed her way.

Mrs. Wright's face flushed as she perched on the edge of a floral settee. "I'm sorry, girls. If I had known he didn't want to propose, I wouldn't have allowed him to step foot in here."

As usual, Mae's sigh accompanied her own, though Mae's was more pronounced.

"I don't understand why you two don't want to get married. Land's sake, every other woman your age has long since hitched their plow with a man. At twenty-five, you'll soon be left with nothing but slim pickings." Mrs. Wright fanned herself with the apron. "Mercy, it's hot in here. I never understood why my Homer wanted to live in Texas. Give me the East Coast any day."

Mae sat beside the portly woman. "Do you still have family back east?"

Mrs. Wright shook her head. "I wish. I'd sell this place in a heartbeat and head back there if I did. Nope. I'm stuck here like you girls."

Ellie didn't contradict the woman, but they were far from being stuck. They happened to like the warm climate and the opportunity to be in charge of their own destinies. That was certainly better than being bounced back and forth like a kite on the wind. No thank you. They had no desire to return to their past. Ellie sucked the memories back where they belonged—in the deep cortex of her brain.

"I do wonder where the fella came from though." Mrs. Wright continued to fan herself. "I haven't seen him before. Course, there's word around town that old man Rogers' son inherited his spread, just south of town. Maybe it's him."

"Odd he didn't introduce himself." Ellie glanced at the door.

Mae lifted an eyebrow. "Why would you care if he told us his name?"

She studied her twin for a second and then shrugged. Should they have given him a chance to explain more instead of shooing him out the door?

Mae's eyes narrowed. "You're awful quiet, Ellie. Something wrong?"

"What? No."

Mae stared at her. "You aren't thinking—?"

"Don't be silly. Of course not." Ellie crossed to the window and peered out at the silent street. The stranger was long gone. She turned away, avoiding eye contact with her sister.

"Silly me." Mrs. Wright shoved herself to her feet. "Here I am sitting and jawing when I should be checking on our supper before it burns."

"I'll help you." Mae stood. "Are you coming, Ellie?"

If she refused, Mae would barrage her with questions once they returned to the comfort of their room. She nodded, unsure why the cowboy's visit had stirred such unease within her and prayed her sister wouldn't pick up on it.

What had the man really wanted? Did he really desire a cook and not a wife? Could she sneak behind Mae's back and find out more about him? Ellie thrust thoughts of the tall cowboy as far away as possible.

***

Luke Rogers's stomach roared as he kneed his mare toward home. Smelling the chicken frying in the boardinghouse had been pure torture. If only he could live there just for the

15

night so he could eat a decent meal. Worst of all, he'd failed his mission and would have to answer to his men when he returned to the ranch.

Too bad the Good Fixin's Diner only stayed open for breakfast and lunch. Didn't they know a body had a hankering for an evening meal too? Actually, he had a hankering for any decent meal. He and his men hadn't had one since Leroy upped and left two weeks ago. He stole away in the dead of night leaving nothing behind but a note saying he'd got hitched and was returning east with his new wife.

No warning. No suggestions for a replacement cook to feed a bunkhouse full of hungry men. Men who weren't going to be happy when Luke returned home without a cook in tow.

Luke hefted a sigh. He needed to earn the men's trust, or he'd soon have a mutiny on his hands. They already questioned his authority. Had ever since he took over his father's spread a month ago.

A heavy weight pressed on his chest. He'd never had time to say good-bye to his pa or make things right. Instead, the gulf of their last argument stretched between here and heaven with no way for Luke to ask Pa for forgiveness.

His mare snorted and picked up her pace as the ranch came into view. At least she'd have a decent supper, but he couldn't say the same for him and his men.

"Howdy, Luke," Bart greeted. The old timer had been Pa's foreman for as long as Luke could remember. "How'd it go, boy?" He clapped Luke on the back as soon as he dismounted.

Luke chewed on the inside of his cheek. Might as well fess up. The men would know soon enough. "She said no."

"You don't say." Bart tilted his Stetson. "I heard those two can be a handful. They give you what for and send you packing?"

Luke grunted. "Something like that." He chose to leave out the part where the landlady swatted him like a fly. He untied the cinch and heaved the saddle over a rail in the barn, picking up a brush on his way to the doorway.

Bart unbridled Lady and hung the bridle on a hook.

"I don't suppose one of the fellas made any chow?" Luke brushed even strokes across Lady's back.

Bart leaned against a fence post. "They were counting on you to bring a cook home."

"Guess I'm making grub again." Luke's gut clenched at the thought.

"Fellas won't be too happy about that. Too bad your mama never taught you to cook." Bart snickered.

"If you remember, I spent most of my days riding beside you and Pa." Luke chucked the brush into a wooden box just inside the barn and then stepped outside to open the fence to the pasture. Lady trotted past and joined the other horses grazing in the field.

"Too bad your mama never had a gal. Maybe if you had a sister, she'd take pity on you and move back home to cook." Bart rubbed a hand across his gray whiskers. "Course you could always marry a gal, so we'd have our bellies full each night."

Luke pinned his foreman with a glare. "You know that's not going to happen, especially after..."

Bart held up a hand. "Never mind, boy. I didn't mean to bring up bad memories." He fell into step with Luke as they headed to the bunkhouse. "We'll think of something."

They slipped into the long wooden building and every man's head swung in their direction. Might as well fess up before they started asking questions. "I haven't been able to secure a cook yet."

The men grumbled.

"I'll have something ready for you all in two shakes."

"That's what we're afraid of, boss." Slim Williams stood. "Every time I eat yer cookin' I end up with a bellyache."

Several cowpokes echoed similar sentiments.

Luke didn't stay to hear the rest of their complaints. He meandered into the small kitchen and started opening up a mess of cans of beans. The fellas wouldn't be happy with the simple meal, but surely he couldn't ruin the plain fare.

He dumped the beans into a pot and shoved it onto the hottest part of the stove. He threw in a couple logs for extra measure. Soon sweat dripped from his nose and sizzled when it hit the hot stove. A strange smell filled the air.

The beans! He grabbed the pot and cried out. Pain seared through the palm of his hand and down to his fingertips. His grip slipped, and the pan dropped to the wooden floor with a loud clunk before tipping on its side and spilling their supper all over the dirty boards.

Luke checked over his shoulder. Nobody had come to investigate yet. He grabbed a spoon and a rag from the table. With the cloth covering his pulsating hand, he loosely grasped the handle and scooped beans back in the pot.

He made sure to avoid the clods of dirt and manure. Most of the meal could be salvaged. He prayed the fellas wouldn't notice any strange tastes in their supper. He shoved the spoon into the pot and grabbed the handle with his good hand as he carried the beans to the table in the main room of the bunkhouse.

"Grub's on the table."

The men congregated like vultures on a dead deer. They grumbled about having to eat beans again but scooped the meal into their bowls. After a simple prayer, they dug in. They didn't talk. Only slurping sounds and metal spoons scraping against dishes filled the room.

"Hey, what's this?" Slim held up his spoon with a suspicious clod hanging from it.

Luke swallowed. He thought he'd avoided every speck of manure. Apparently he had missed one. He closed his eyes. Come tomorrow he'd do whatever it took to convince the cook from Good Fixin's Diner to fill in until he could find a permanent replacement.

Chapter Two

Jed Davis poked his head into the kitchen where Ellie worked. "There's a fella out front who says he has to see you."

Perspiration trickled down her face and onto her high-neck dress. Spicy steam wafted from the chili pot as she stirred it. She tugged at the button of the limp collar she'd starched the night before and released it, letting in blessed air. Mercy. She should've known better than to wear the garment to work.

Jed tapped a pencil against the small notepad he used to write meal orders for his diner. "He said he won't leave until you come out and talk to him."

Ellie grabbed a spatula and flipped a steak sizzling in the pan, then added her secret seasonings. She wiped her hands on the apron at her waist and shoved a pin back into her hair. The noon rush hour always made it look like a bird had built a nest in it.

"Keep an eye on that steak so it doesn't burn, or old man Minter won't be happy." Her gaze flitted around the kitchen. "The cobbler's about ready to be taken out and—"

"Jist get out there and tell the fella you aren't interested, so you can take care of all this."

Ellie mentally listed all the unfinished orders that required attending to before pushing through the swinging door. Once she stepped into the dining room, she realized she hadn't asked Jed who the fellow was.

She greeted those who called out to her as she wove through the room, taking note of the tables that needed to be cleaned or to have fresh flowers added. Her eyes caught those of a tall cowboy. The same cowboy from Mrs. Wright's parlor the night before. Persistent.

He stood by the front door, twirling his hat in his hands. Ellie hid the smile that longed to break out.

"Howdy, miss." He stepped closer and held out a hand. "I didn't get the chance to introduce myself last night. Name's Luke Rogers."

His large, calloused hand gripped hers for a fraction of a second. The warmth of his fingers lingered after he released his grasp. "Ellie, uh, Stafford." Her brain and tongue weren't working together.

He nodded. "Mind if we sit for a few minutes?" He headed toward an empty table and pulled a chair out for her.

Ellie perched on the edge of the seat. "I told you last night I'm not interested in marriage."

"Then we should get along right fine, because I'm not either." A shadow passed across his eyes.

She waited for him to elaborate, but he didn't.

"Bottom line, I'm in desperate need of a cook."

"I already have a job."

He leaned forward. "I'm willing to double whatever you make here."

"You don't even know what that is."

"Don't matter. I've got to have you, and I'm not leaving without you."

"Excuse me?" Ellie pushed back against the wooden spindles of the seat.

Color crept into his cheeks and across his broad forehead. "I didn't mean...that is, I only need you as a *cook* until I can find someone permanent. A fill in."

Ellie licked her lips. "I work here five days a week. Breakfast and lunch, and I have no desire to leave."

Luke's lips pursed and he ran a hand through his blond curls. One lock of hair danced across his forehead and hung there. Ellie resisted the urge to tuck it back in place. She shook her head. Must have been in the heat of the kitchen too long.

"I've been here since first thing this morning, and I'm not leaving until you say yes."

Ellie shot out of her seat. "Guess you'll be here when Jed locks up then." She started to turn, but his hand on her arm stopped her. The warmth of his fingers scorched through the sleeve of her dress like a splash of hot grease.

"Is this fella bothering ya, Ellie?" Jed stood two feet away with his arms barreled across his broad chest.

A surge of relief blazed through Ellie. She broke Luke's grip on her, and ducked behind Jed. Since when had she become such a coward? She'd always been the strong one.

She backed her way toward the kitchen, unable to break the connection of her locked stare with Luke.

"Hey, Jed," the blacksmith hollered from the far corner, "what's a man gotta do to get you to take his order?"

Luke's gaze flitted in that direction and Ellie darted into the kitchen. Her heart pounded as she leaned against the door frame. Never had a man had such an effect on her.

***

Luke slipped along the edge of the dining room keeping an eye on Ellie's enforcer. A customer occupied Jed for the moment. With a quick glance over his shoulder, Luke pushed open the door through which Ellie had disappeared.

Once inside, he leaned against the door frame and watched as the woman scurried about the room. She forked a juicy steak onto a plate along with a steaming baked potato and a mess of green beans. Then she bent and withdrew a cobbler from the oven. His mouth watered, though he'd already had a healthy portion of the same meal and dessert. She set the cobbler on the counter, then picked up a long-handled spoon and stirred the pot of chili, bringing a spoonful to her lips for a taste. It was at that exact moment that she spotted him. A strange sensation traveled through him, one he recognized and didn't welcome. He shoved it back down.

The spoon dropped from her grasp, splattered the front of her flowered apron leaving a bright stain, and clattered to the floor. Her face blanched.

"I'm not going to hurt you, Miss Stafford."

She opened her mouth, probably to call out to the big bruiser in the dining room. He inched forward. "I need a cook, miss. Even if you can only come out for one meal a day, my men would appreciate it."

He held out his bandaged hand to her. "Please consider it."

Her doe-colored eyes studied his hand. "What happened?"

Heat flared on his neck as the scene from the night before flickered through his mind. He tucked his hand into his pocket. "Pot of beans was hotter than I figured on."

Her eyes narrowed and an eyebrow quirked. "You've been cooking?"

He scowled. "Why do you find it unbelievable?"

She smiled and her eyes twinkled. "It's not very often I find a man who can cook."

Luke snorted. "That's the problem. I can't. I'm about ready to have a revolt on my hands if I don't figure something out soon. Chow's important to a fella."

"Are you still willing to pay double if I only cook the evening meal? I won't leave Jed in the lurch, and I made a promise to him to stay here."

He nodded. If he could eat her food for only one meal a day, he'd do about anything. Well, except marry the gal. No sirree. He had no intention on traveling that road again.

"How far from town do you live?" She sliced the cobbler into equal portions and scooped one onto a plate.

"About a mile or so."

"How will I find your place?" She ladled a generous portion of chili into a bowl and added a blob of something. He couldn't tell what.

"I can take you out there the first time and bring you back." Luke sucked in a deep breath. "Could you start right after you're through with the noon meal?"

She nibbled on her lip and stopped her constant activity for a few seconds. "And you have no hidden ambitions toward marriage because if you do—"

"Never!" The word flew from his mouth like sour grapes.

Her eyes flew open.

"A cook. No strings attached."

"You'll start looking for a replacement for me right away?"

"Agreed." He held out his hand.

She hesitated before slipping her small hand into his. "I expect to be paid at the end of each week." She mumbled a sum and his breath faltered.

He'd be dipping into Pa's savings to keep her, but she just might be the answer to his prayers.

***

Mae was going to kill her. Ellie would have to explain that working for Luke was no different than working for Jed. But then, Jed was over twice the age of Luke and didn't have big blue eyes and expansive shoulders. Her gaze flitted toward his before she lowered them and worked on filling another plate of food.

A blaze of heat scurried up her neck. Since when did she care about those things? She and

28

her twin sister had been chasing away men for as long as Ellie could remember. Not that Luke had any intentions toward her, which made it a perfect situation. She could perform the job for him while still enjoying the company of a handsome gentleman. At least she assumed he was a gentleman. He hadn't given her any indication he wasn't.

"What are you doing in here?" Jed's voiced boomed through the small kitchen. He jabbed a finger into Luke's muscled arm. "I told you to stop bothering the lady."

Luke towered a good four inches over Jed, but that didn't stop her boss from glaring at the cowboy.

"He's not bothering me."

Jed's mouth gaped. "Never thought I'd see the day when you'd finally get interested in a fella. It's about time."

The tell tale warmth crept up her face. Maybe Jed would blame it on working in the kitchen on a hot day.

"It ain't nothing like that." Luke stretched an inch taller. "I'm here to hire her."

Jed glowered. "I'm not going to let some little whippersnapper steal my best gal away from me."

A chuckle burst from Ellie's lips, and both men turned toward her. "No need to get your ropes tied in a knot. Luke and I already discussed this, and there's no reason why I can't work for both of you."

"You aren't leaving me?" Jed's gaze swung to hers. "That's different then."

Jed clapped Luke on the back.

Men. Ellie would never figure them out, nor did she plan to try.

"Does Mae know about him?" Jed nodded his head in the cowboy's direction.

"Not exactly."

Luke swiveled toward her.

"You best get these dinners out there before your customers send a search party." Ellie handed the loaded platter to her boss. "Never mind about Mae. I'll smooth things over with her."

Jed studied her before he disappeared through the door to the dining room.

"Is there something I should know?" Luke asked.

Ellie shook her head. He wouldn't understand even if she knew how to explain it to him. She didn't think anyone else could fully comprehend what it meant to be a twin, let alone twins with the past they had. No. This was something she'd have to deal with herself.

Her chest tightened. It would be the first time a man had come between her and her sister, and it had nothing to do with a potential beau. Unfortunately, Ellie feared that's how Mae would see it. She shifted away to check on the chili.

Luke fidgeted with his shirt collar. "You aren't backing out on me, are you?"

Moisture pricked the corner of her eyes, and she blinked it away.

"Miss?"

"Ellie."

She bent over, placed a pan of prepared dough into the oven, and prayed for composure.

"Ellie? You didn't answer my question." She could hear the uncertainty in his voice.

She swallowed and took a deep breath. "A Stafford doesn't go back on a promise." *No matter what.*

Chapter Three

Ellie blew out the lamp and crept up the stairs. She shifted to the side on the sixth step so it wouldn't creak and wake the entire household, then inched her way toward the bedroom she shared with Mae. A sliver of light shone beneath the door. Mae was still up. Ellie had hoped this confrontation wouldn't occur until morning. She fumbled with the latch, then squared her shoulders and pushed the door open.

Mae sat on the bed with her arms crossed. Her cheeks were flushed. "Where have you been? I've been worried something fierce."

Ellie cleared her throat and started undressing. "I was with Luke."

"Luke?" Mae scowled. "Who is Luke and since when do you call men by their first name?"

Ellie hung her dress on a peg, straightening the length of the skirt. "How was work at the dress shop today?"

"You're avoiding me. What's going on?" The bed's ropes popped and groaned. Mae'd probably stood, but Ellie didn't want to turn around yet. She bent and unbuttoned her shoes, kicking them to the side.

She slipped a nightgown over her head and gathered her courage. Ellie inhaled a deep breath and said, "Luke is the cowboy who stopped by yesterday."

"What? When did you see him?" Hurt cracked her sister's voice.

"Oh, Mae, don't be angry with me." Ellie turned and gripped her sister's hand. "He stopped by the diner earlier. In fact, he stayed for both meals and wouldn't leave until I spoke with him."

"We promised."

"This has nothing to do with our promise. You know I wouldn't break that." Ellie studied her twin's face. "The poor man has been without a cook for his men for two weeks now."

"I don't understand why that has anything to do with you. You already have a good job at the diner. Why would you want to leave it? Jed's been good to you. Probably the first man who has been since Pa." Mae scooted to the edge of the bed.

Ellie joined her. "That's the thing. I'll still be working at the diner. I'll cook at the ranch for supper only."

"I don't understand."

"I couldn't refuse him when I saw his burnt hand. You should have seen the damage he'd done trying to make a meal for his men."

Mae's lips twitched. "You always did have a soft spot for anything injured."

A vision of all the kids who'd come to her at the orphanage flashed across her mind. Each one needing a bandage and a hug. Years ago, Ellie'd had desires of becoming a physician, but poor orphan children didn't have the means to do something like that. And the fact that she was a girl only made the ambition that much more futile. She blew out a sigh. Her dream was best forgotten.

Mrs. Franklin, the head matron, had always said God hadn't intended for Ellie to fill her head with such nonsense as medicine and science. The woman had stated she was better suited using the gifts God had given her. She should cook for others. Mrs. Franklin had been all about serving folks. Not that it was a bad thing, but Ellie'd always wanted more in her life than just cooking.

"Ellie?"

Tears pricked her eyes, but she blinked them away. "You're right. I can't stand to see someone hurt. It's partly why I took the position. I felt sorry for Luke. Besides, the job is only until he can hire someone permanent."

"You aren't planning to keep on, then?" Mae scooched up against the pillows, bent her knees, and rested her chin on them.

Ellie shook her head. "No reason to fear, my dear. You and I are in this together, and nothing will ever separate us."

"You're sure?" Mae studied her.

Ellie refused to flinch under her sister's scrutiny. She had nothing to hide. "Of course. Let's get some sleep. Morning will be here before we know it."

"Good night, Ellie. I love you." Mae slid underneath the sheet.

Ellie slithered into bed beside her sister and yawned. "I love you too, Mae. Good night." She reached over and blew out the lantern on the nightstand.

Minutes later her sister's breathing became steady as she slipped into sleep.

Ellie tossed as she thought about how polite Luke had been when he'd introduced her to his men. He'd made a point to say he expected them to treat her like a lady. No other man had done that before, except for Jed, but he didn't count. The diner owner was old enough to be her father.

Her memories of Pa were rusty. He'd died when they were six. Ma had done her best keeping them together and trying to make ends meet. She'd worked two jobs to put food on their table and keep the bank from foreclosing on their small farm. Even with the fields hired out to their neighbor, life had been a struggle. And then Ma had gotten ill. She wasn't able to shake it no matter how hard Ellie had tried to nurse her back to health.

Ellie had awakened in the middle of the night to check on Ma. Her mother's chilled form told the tale. She'd died sometime after they'd kissed her goodnight.

A tear trickled down Ellie's cheek. If only she'd known how to help her. If only they'd had the money to buy the medicine she'd needed. If only Ma hadn't gotten ill in the first place. She'd said it was just a summer cold, and she'd be better in no time. If only she'd been right.

Why did you have to take them both, Lord? Her silent question bounced off the ceiling and like always, no answer came. Ellie turned over and tried to forget about God abandoning them. And she tried not to think about a pair of big blue eyes and a head full of blond curls.

***

Luke tossed on his bed. For the first time in over two weeks he had a full belly so he couldn't blame his restlessness on hunger pains. If anything, his gut was happy with the three delicious meals he'd had. Two at the diner and the other when Ellie worked her first supper at the ranch. Boy, that gal could cook. Bringing her to the ranch had been the right decision. Too bad she couldn't cook all of their meals. They'd be eating like kings if she did. Of course, if she had a permanent position, the men might get sluggish and not want to do their work.

He rolled over on the bed he'd had since childhood. Somehow when he'd come back to the ranch after being away for a few years, it hadn't seemed right to take up residence in his parents' unused bedroom. His old one suited him just fine. Besides, he didn't want to try and sleep in a room that would only bring back the regrets he had with Pa.

Luke punched his pillow and shifted positions again. He'd better get some shut-eye, or he'd be dragging tomorrow when they moved the herd to the higher pasture. They needed rain soon. He prayed the watering holes wouldn't dry up.

His brain flitted back and forth between the concerns of owning a ranch and the pair of brown eyes that had met his when he'd complimented her on the meal tonight. It had been strange having a woman in the bunkhouse. But it had also seemed right.

"Enough, Rogers. Get to sleep." His mumbled admonition did little to settle his restless mind. Sleep was long in coming.

***

Ellie hurried through the kitchen cleanup, humming as she worked. She dried the last pot and put it away. Everything was in its place. She stepped in the dining area and wiped each of the tables.

"You're in a good mood." Jed leaned against the doorframe. "It wouldn't have to do with a tall cowboy, would it?"

Heat flushed up Ellie's cheeks. "Don't be silly. It's just a beautiful day."

Jed grunted. "It's hotter than an oven, and you know it."

Ellie smiled. "The sun's shining and the birds are singing."

Jed shook his head. "Guess I'd better start advertising for a new cook."

Her head swung up from her task. "What? Why?"

"Cause you got it bad."

"What are you talking about? I merely mentioned it's a beautiful day." She hadn't said one word about Luke. Hadn't thought about him, either. At least not in the last few minutes. "I have no intention of leaving you."

Jed scratched his whiskered face. "We'll see. I still say I need to keep my eye out for someone to take over your position."

Ellie planted her hands on her hips. "Don't be silly."

Jed stared at her and shook his head.

"I best be on my way. I'll see you in the morning." Ellie gathered her knitting basket and headed for the door. The bell chimed as she stepped onto the boarded walkway. The sweltering heat nearly took her breath away. She hurried to the stable.

"Howdy, Miss Stafford. I've got a mare all ready for you." The livery owner led a horse toward her.

"Thank you," Ellie said as she mounted. She adjusted her skirts and hung the basket over the horn.

"Sorry I don't have a side saddle. We don't have much need for them here."

"That's fine." Ellie flicked him a coin instead of handing it to him, afraid that in the process of bending over she'd lose her seat. She pulled back on the reins like he'd shown her earlier that morning when he'd given her a quick lesson on how to ride.

Her heart galloped in her throat.

"You gonna be fine by yourself?"

She nodded as the horse started moving, not wanting to let go of the reins and wave. Her heart slowed from its erratic pattering as she learned the gentle rhythm of sitting in the saddle and how to flow with the horse instead of bouncing in the saddle opposite of the mare's pace. She'd considered renting a small conveyance each day but hated to pay the extra money when a single beast was far cheaper.

Surely riding a horse couldn't be that difficult to learn.

Besides, if her current situation was any indication, she was a natural. Ellie smiled as the dips and swells of the land passed, and she drew closer to the ranch. Who knew that riding could be so empowering? She'd have to share it with Mae on their next day off together.

She switched the reins to one hand, opened her woven basket, and searched through the contents for her small mirror. She'd been in such a hurry to leave the diner that she'd forgotten to take note of her appearance and fix whatever damage had occurred from working in the hot kitchen.

Not that she cared what Luke thought of her. Her mother had instilled in them from an early age that a lady always made sure she was presentable.

Ellie shifted the knitting needles out of the way and dug to the bottom of her bag. The mare threw her head and pranced sideways. The reins slipped from Ellie's hand. Her heart plummeted as the horse increased speed. The landscape blurred as they raced forward.

She leaned over and held tight to the saddle, not knowing where else to grip. Her knees dug into the side of the mare. A tree limb whipped across her cheek, followed by a sting.

The horse stepped into a dip, throwing Ellie forward in the saddle.

She clung to the mane, her fingers locking through the dark hair. Her legs trembled as they clenched tight around the horse's ribs.

The mare shrieked and tossed her head again. Ellie's fingers slipped.

Her body jolted with each gallop, tossing her back and forth on the saddle, like a toy boat, heaved and thrown on a stormy sea.

Dear God, help me.

The mare continued her frantic pace. A wooden fence loomed a mere fifty yards in front of them.

Closer. Closer.

Ellie screamed when the mare halted, and she went sailing through the air and landed with a bone-crunching thud. Every muscle in her body throbbed before the world turned black.

Chapter Four

Luke's heart launched into his throat as Ellie swooped through the air and landed with a loud thump. He spurred his mount into motion, crossing the meadow in record time. His Stetson flew off in the wild pursuit. He reined his horse to a halt, slid from the saddle, and knelt beside the woman's still form. A bright red laceration marred her pale face.

"Ellie?" He knelt in the dirt, afraid to move her. His fingers hovered before he lightly squeezed her shoulder. "Ellie, speak to me."

She moaned and touched her forehead.

Alive! Thank you, Lord.

"What happened?"

"Best I can tell, something spooked your horse."

Her eyes flicked open, and she squinted into the bright sunlight before groaning and struggling to a seated position. "My head hurts something fierce."

"Don't move too fast. You might have broken something."

Her fingers explored the sore spot on her cheek. "I don't think so. I do feel like my body's been pummeled by the wheels of a stage coach though. Give me a hand."

She placed her slim hand into his calloused one. So small. He swallowed and tugged her to standing, his arm snaking around her waist to steady her when she wobbled. The scent of roses wafted over him. His jaw tightened.

"Why did the horse throw me like that?" Her body trembled as she stared at the mare and shrunk closer to his side. "She isn't going to attack, is she?"

He chuckled. "Never heard of an attack horse before. Come on. The best thing you can do when you're thrown is to get back up again."

She dug her heels in and tugged her hand out of his. "No, sir. I'm not getting on there again. Once was enough."

He glanced at the horse and then back at Ellie. "What do you mean, once is enough? You've ridden before, haven't you?"

She shook her head. Fear blazed in her eyes.

A lump formed in his throat. *Dear God, she could've been killed because I was too busy to fetch her.*

"I just assumed you knew how to ride." He shoved his fingers through his hair. "It's my fault."

Ellie swallowed and gripped his forearm. "You couldn't have known." She studied the dirt for a moment before meeting his gaze. "I didn't want you to think...that is...I didn't want to be an imposition. Mae would say I let my pride get in the way. I should have said something...shouldn't have been searching for my..." Her cheeks flamed.

The warmth of her fingertips branded his arm, and he didn't want to move. What had she been searching for? Was her jumbled speech a result of a crack to her noggin?

A chill blew across his arm when she broke the connection. Her head dipped, and she wouldn't meet his eyes. He scrubbed a hand over his face.

He hopped over the fence and murmured words to comfort the skittish mare as he slowly approached her. "Whoa, girl. What's got you all edgy?" He ran his hand along her side and saw two puncture marks near the saddle. The horse flesh rippled beneath his fingers. What could have caused it?

Luke lifted the basket from the horn and rooted through it.

"What are you doing? Those are my personal things." Ellie edged up to the opposite side of the fence. Fire danced in her eyes.

He yanked out the long pointed needles. A ball of yarn tumbled out with them and bounced to the dirt. He held up the needles and said, "Were you looking for these while riding a horse you had no business being on in the first place?"

***

Anger rippled across Luke's face, and a muscle twitched in his jaw. Ellie took a tiny step backward. Telling him she'd been looking for her mirror and not her knitting would further upset him. Best to say nothing.

While she might agree that she shouldn't have been riding the horse, it galled her to hear him say it. She ducked under the wooden beam and crawled through the fence. Ellie gathered her courage, yanked her belongings from Luke's outstretched hand, and stuffed them back into her basket. She slung it over her arm.

She hesitated a moment, then scooped up the reins and tugged the horse to follow her...back to town. Good riddance. She had no need of his job anyway.

"Where do you think you're going?"

"Home." She trudged along, avoiding a prickly pear cactus.

"I guess we'll just starve. Didn't know we were cutting into your valuable knitting time."

She pinned him with a glare.

His footsteps pounded against the packed earth, and he soon came abreast of her. "Please, wait." Luke pinched his lips together to keep from spewing his frustration.

He didn't say anything for a minute but the muscle in his jaw continued to twitch. "Look, I'm sorry. When I saw you sailing through the air..." His Adam's apple bobbed. "I should have provided transportation for you, one way or another. This is on me, not you."

Her conscience nipped at her. She shouldn't have been distracted while riding.

"The truth is, I need you."

Other than Mae and her parents, nobody had ever needed her. Not that the man was searching for a wife, nor did she have a desire to be one.

When she and her sister were younger, folks had been interested in adopting just one girl, never two. They'd always been interested in Mae, not her. Probably because her twin had inherited Ma's demureness while Ellie was far too rough-and-tumble to suit most potential new parents.

"Please don't leave me." Redness worked its way up his neck and into his face. "I mean me and the fellas."

Of course. It was all about filling their guts. Best she remember that and not get any crazy notions.

"I'll make sure you're seen safely back and forth each day from here on out." He cocked his head while staring at her face. "Let's get that cut taken care of."

She glanced toward town. It would make for a long walk, especially when her body ached all over. Her gaze swung back to his and she nodded, not trusting her voice. He tugged the reins from her fingers and held out an arm. Her heart thudded as they strolled toward the bunkhouse.

Silence greeted them as they stepped inside the cool interior. She'd expected a cowboy or two to put in an appearance, but they must all be busy elsewhere. Ellie swallowed. She hadn't counted on being alone with the man.

"You sit there and I'll fetch some salve."

She sat on the edge of a wooden bench. Last night she'd been so busy with meal preparations she hadn't taken time to look around. A line of beds stood along both sides of the long building, with a small trunk at the foot of each one. Clothes were strewn across every spare space, even dotting the dirty floor.

"Here we go." Luke dragged a chair over and plopped onto it. He dunked a rag into a bowl of water. "This might sting a little."

She sucked in a breath as a slew of sewing needles pricked her cheek as he washed the laceration.

"Sorry."

He dabbed it dry with a clean cloth and opened a tin.

Ellie wrinkled her nose at the odor wafting from the small container. "What is that? It's smells awful."

"Salve I use on the horses when they get injured."

"You are *not* going to use that on me." Ellie drew back.

"Why not? It works great. The fellas and I use it all the time."

"You can't be serious."

"Stop your fussin' and sit still."

Before she could protest, he swiped a healthy amount onto her cheek. Her stomach roiled at the stench.

"It don't smell too great, but your face will be as smooth as a newborn in a couple days. You'll see." His light touch on her cheek as he scraped off the extra residue caused a swarm of butterflies in her innards.

His eyes met hers before his gaze dropped to her lips.

She shot out of her seat. "I best get busy." Without a backward glance, she darted into the small kitchen.

She rolled up her sleeves, then started peeling potatoes, her mind far from her task. While the pot simmered and before the steaks needed attention, her fingers flew as she knit a hat to send back to the Children's Aid Society. Anything to keep her mind off the handsome rancher and his gentle fingers.

***

Ellie crept up the steps later that night, the familiar light glowing under her door. She opened it and yawned.

Mae took one look at her and gasped. "Ellie, what happened?" She sprung out of bed and stood beside her. Her nose wrinkled. "And what's that awful odor?"

"It's me." She sank down on the side of the bed and started unbuttoning her shoes. "I had a run-in with my horse. Apparently it didn't take kindly to being poked with knitting needles."

"You rode a horse by yourself? Why would you do something like that? What happened? How did you get the scratch and why are you moving so stiffly?" Mae's questions made Ellie's temples throb.

Dear, curious Mae. All Ellie wanted to do was crawl under the covers and get some sleep...and not think about Luke. Or her aching body.

She told her sister about the run-in with the horse as she undressed and slipped a nightgown over her head, deliberately leaving out the part about Luke taking care of the scratch. And his lingering fingers on her face. She needed time to sort through her emotions concerning the encounter and didn't know if Mae would understand. How could she explain something to her sister when she didn't comprehend it herself? Somehow it didn't seem right keeping something like this from her twin either. She shoved her thoughts back to where they belonged...in the far recesses of her brain.

"I can't figure out why you tried to ride all the way to wherever he lives when you have no experience with horses. What were you thinking?" Mae settled into bed beside her.

Ellie yawned again. "I didn't want to spend the extra money on renting a buggy. Thought I could do it myself."

"You always were braver than me. I don't think I would've even hired a conveyance." Mae blew out the lantern on her side of the bed. "I probably would have walked or insisted he provided transportation."

Ellie pinned her sister with a stare. "You wouldn't have made any such demands."

Mae chuckled. "Probably not, but I would've at least thought about doing so."

"Thinking and doing are two different things." Ellie snuggled under the sheet and moaned. "I think I'm going to be hurting something fierce come morning."

"Too bad Mrs. Wright only lets us bathe every other week. Even with the lack of rain lately, it'd be nice to soak more often. The pitcher and basin do an adequate job between times, but not when—"

"You ache all over." Ellie finished her sister's sentence. Back at the orphanage the other children could never understand how the sisters often knew what the other was thinking or going to say.

"Hmm. Maybe I can do something about that," Mae said.

"What are you talking about?" Ellie struggled to keep her eyes open.

"Never you mind. Sleep, sister, and leave the rest up to me." Mae patted her arm.

This time Ellie had no clue what her twin was thinking, nor did she have the strength to ponder it. "G'night."

She drifted to sleep, dreaming about being vaulted off a horse and caught by a handsome rancher. His arms wrapped around her body and held her tight. He tucked her hair behind her ear and whispered words of assurance about never allowing harm to come to her. He said that he knew from the get-go she was the perfect woman for him, as long as she learned how to ride a horse.

Then he dropped her to the ground, saying she'd failed the test. Any woman who couldn't keep her seat on a gentle horse had no business being a rancher's wife. She was good enough as a cook, but that was it.

The rancher turned his back and rode into the sunset without a backward glance.

Chapter Five

Ellie woke with a sob.

"What's the matter?" Mae touched her arm.

She shifted slightly. Pain shot through every pore of her body. "Ohh. I hurt everywhere."

"From the horse, or do you think you're catching something too?"

Ellie shook her head and then regretted the movement. "Never knew it could hurt so much, being thrown like that."

"I don't think you hurt from the throwing but the landing." Mae smiled. "Stay right there, I'll take care of everything."

She couldn't have moved if she wanted to.

Her sister scurried back into their room a minute later. "I've convinced Mrs. Wright to allow you a hot bath. She's heating the water now." Mae glanced at the timepiece pinned to her dress. "I'll need to head to the dress shop in a few minutes."

Ellie's eyes fluttered as she half-listened to her twin mumbling to herself. Something about being chilly and a buggy, which made no sense. Mae had never loved the cold winters of New York like she had.

Ellie had especially enjoyed their years on the farm when the snow drifted halfway up Pa's waist. Sometimes he'd secured a rope between the house and the barn so as not to lose his way in the snowstorms.

"I don't think you need to worry about being cold here." She yawned and shifted on the bed. At least today was her day off at the diner so she could sleep longer. Somehow between now and this afternoon she'd have to figure out the best way to get dressed without hurting.

"It's perfect." Mae grinned.

"Hmm?" Ellie struggled to lift her head. "What did you say?"

"You rest, dear, and I'll have Mrs. Wright fetch you when the bath water is ready." Her sister patted her cheek. "Wish me well."

"Well with what?" Since when did Mae ask for well-wishes before she headed to her job as a seamstress?

***

Luke scanned the woman on the wagon seat beside him. He reached over, his fingers grazing her cheek. "I've never seen a scratch heal as fast as that."

She shifted and stared straight ahead.

"You feelin'...I mean are you sore from your fall?"

Again no response.

Strange. Had he done something to offend Ellie the night before? She had been a might off on their ride back to town, but he'd attributed it to her being sore from her run-in with the horse.

He flicked his wrist, urging the team to increase their pace. Quiet filled their ride to the ranch. When they arrived, he hopped down and came around to help Ellie. His hands gripped her waist as he swung her to the ground. A small squeak escaped her lips.

"Sorry. I'm sure you're hurting." He stepped back but couldn't stop himself from studying her beautiful eyes. He gripped his fingers so he wouldn't reach out to touch her delicate face again.

"I best get started on the meal." She turned toward his house.

Heat soared up his body. "Where you going?"

"Why, to fix supper. What else would I be here for?"

Confusion lined her face. How hard had she hit her head yesterday? He pointed to the bunkhouse. "Aren't you going to cook in there where you've been the past few days?"

"Mercy me, what am I thinking?" She held a cloth bag tight against her chest.

He studied her as she marched to the building, her shoulders stiff. Something was off, but he couldn't figure what. She didn't move like her muscles were complaining from being thrown yesterday or maybe she was good at hiding it. He shook his head and hopped onto the wagon and drove it to the barn.

"You got it bad, boy." Bart shook his head.

"What're you talking about?" Luke unhitched the horses from the wagon.

Bart nodded toward the bunkhouse. "You're startin' to fall for her, ain't you?"

"What? No!" He unbuckled the bridles and hung them on a hook just inside the barn door.

"Nothin' wrong with fallin' in love again." Bart patted the back of one of the horses.

"You know I have no such plans. Not after—"

"Gotta let it go, boy. Don't let bitterness rule your life. Just 'cause one gal disappointed you don't mean this one will."

He bit back a grunt. "Never said I had an interest in Ellie."

Bart clapped him on the back. "You didn't have to. It's written all across your face whenever the two of you are together."

His breathing hitched in his chest. The foreman didn't know what he was talking about.

"Not every gal is gonna take your money and leave you standin' at the altar."

Luke stopped grooming his horse and glared at Bart. "Since when did I ask you to get involved in my business?"

Bart met his stare with one of his own. "You didn't. But you have to let it go, or it'll eat you alive."

"Should have listened to Pa."

His foreman came to his side and studied his face. "You know he forgave you."

Luke's last conversation with Pa flooded his mind. His father had warned him that the gal he'd asked to marry was only after his money, but Luke got angry and left the ranch to set out and prove him wrong. In his stubbornness he lost the gal, his money, and Pa. He hefted a sigh. If only he had listened to his father's advice. He'd always intended to head home and ask for forgiveness, but he never got around to it. Too proud. Kept putting it off, thinking he'd have plenty of time. Until word came that Pa had died.

"Should have been here." Moisture clogged his throat.

"Aw, son, there weren't nothin' you could've done after that bull hit him. He died within minutes. He forgave you long before that anyway. You need to work at forgivin' yourself. The good Lord's already forgiven you too. All you gotta do is make things right with Him."

Was it that simple?

"Don't delay, boy. I think there's a gal who's in need of a good lookin' cowpoke. She just don't know it yet." Bart smiled.

Luke shook his head. "I think you've missed your calling, Bart."

"What's that?"

"Instead of a foreman, you should've been a matchmaker."

Bart guffawed and meandered away, but his words stuck with Luke like sap on a June bug. He couldn't get away from them. Maybe it was high time he did something about it.

When he finished his task, he darted to his house. Inside the cool interior he knelt beside his bed. *Lord, I'm sorry I never made things right with Pa before he died. Forgive me. I don't want to hang onto my bitterness any longer. If you have someone new for me to love, can You make that evident? And can You tell Pa I'm sorry?*

With a lighter heart, he stood. His Bible lay open on the bedside table. He flipped through the pages until he saw a passage he'd underlined years prior. Must have been when Ma'd died.

Hide not thy face far from me; put not thy servant away in anger: thou hast been my help; leave me not, neither forsake me, O God of my salvation. When my father and my mother forsake me, then the LORD will take me up.

Luke flicked away moisture from his eye. *Thank You, Lord, that even though Pa and Ma are gone, You still promise to take me up.*

He ran his fingers across the page then stood and placed the Bible back where it had been. Maybe he should seek out Ellie and see if she needed anything. The thought of it made him smile.

The bunkhouse was quiet when he walked inside. He wrinkled his nose at the scent. Odd, it didn't smell like Ellie's usual savory fare. She hadn't cooked anything bad yet. In fact, all the fellas had raved about her abilities long before he'd sought her out.

No clanging of pans came from the kitchen. In fact, no sounds at all. He crept closer. Had Ellie wandered outside?

Luke stopped when he reached the doorway. She sat with her head bent over a scrap of fabric in her lap. Her needle moved in and out of the material before she took note of his appearance. She jumped to her feet, and the color drained from her face.

He inched closer. "What'cha doing?"

"A little sewing while the chili cooks."

He frowned. "I thought you knitted."

Color shot to her cheeks. "I..."

"Chili, huh? Smells different than I remember you serving the other day at the diner. What did you change?"

"It's my sister's recipe." She twisted her hands and wouldn't meet his eyes.

"Are you fixin' cornbread too?" He crept closer.

Her eyes widened, and she shook her head. "Pie?"

She swallowed. "No, just chili. I hope you don't mind."

"The boys will be disappointed. They rave about your food all day long."

"They do?" She stepped backward until she was pinned against the legs of the chair.

He reached out and cupped her face in his hand. She trembled beneath his touch. Luke dipped his head closer and stared into her eyes.

Anger soared through him. How could he be such a fool to be tricked by a woman again?

"So. Was it your idea or Ellie's to try and fool me?"

***

Ellie paced their small room, checking the window every couple of minutes for Luke's wagon to draw up with Mae. At least she assumed her sister had decided to go in her place since he'd never shown up to take her to the ranch. Had she tried to fool him like when they swapped places as children, or had she told him the truth from the start?

What had they talked about in her absence?

Her pulse quickened as the sound of a vehicle stopping in front of the boardinghouse drifted up from the street. She shrank away from the window, not wanting Luke to see her, although she couldn't resist shifting the curtain a smidgen and peering out.

Strange. He hadn't helped Mae out of the wagon but instead sat with a stony expression on his face while her sister climbed down the side.

Her twin said something to him before she scurried inside. His head swiveled to the very window she peeped out of. Hurt flashed across his face, and her heart plummeted to her toes. Something had gone very wrong.

She swung around when Mae threw their bedroom door open thirty seconds later. Her cheeks were bright red.

"What happened?"

"He knew. I tried to go in your place and not tell him." Mae untied the ribbons to her hat.

Ellie sunk on the foot of the bed. "How? When?"

"Mrs. Beadle allowed me to work a half day so I could fill in for you. For one thing, you should have told me that you cook in the bunkhouse and not his house."

"Is that how he found out?"

Her sister shook her head. "No, I don't think so. I know he was surprised my cheek was healed already."

"Why didn't you tell him the truth?"

Mae's brows puckered up. "I figured he might get angry, and I hate situations like that. Of course, I suppose I should have said something. It would simplify things for you if you didn't have to worry about working two jobs. But then you still would want to wait until he found a full-time cook."

Ellie's pulse quickened as her sister rambled. "What did you say?"

"Nothing. I refused to lie to the man. We always agreed that even when we swapped places with one another, we wouldn't lie."

"I'm surprised you would go in my place, especially after the whole fiasco with—"

"You aren't to speak of it." Mae's cheeks flushed. "Never mind about that." She took a deep breath as if clearing her mind of past memories. "Mr. Rogers is extremely observant."

Her heart pounded so loudly she had difficulty hearing Mae's words. "How did he find out?"

Her twin shrugged. "I don't really know. I was in the kitchen sewing, and the man practically scared me to heaven, sneaking up on me like that. He asked me what I had on the stove. Maybe it's because I didn't fix anything other than chili. You know I can't handle those fancy desserts you make, and I scorch cornbread whenever I try to make a pan, so I knew not to try that."

She stopped to take a breath. "I mean, the man got so close I thought he might kiss me."

Something churned inside Ellie. "H-he did?" Her words came out in a whisper.

Mae lifted an eyebrow and studied her. "You *are* beginning to have feelings for him. I'm sure of it."

Ellie jumped up and regretted the sudden movement. She winced. "Don't be silly. He's merely my boss."

"Uh-huh." Mae continued to stare at her.

"What else did he do?"

Her twin didn't answer right away but instead started preparing for bed. Silence stretched for so long between them, Ellie was afraid her sister would never answer the question.

"He took my face in his hand..."

Ellie's fingers trembled so badly she hid them behind her back. "And?" Surely he hadn't kissed her. Had he?

"He asked me whether it was my idea or yours to fool him by swapping places."

Chapter Six

Ellie's gut quivered and flopped as she wiped down the last table at the diner. Luke was fifteen minutes late. Did he intend to come today and pick her up or could he be angry about Mae filling in for her yesterday? There had to be a hundred reasons why he hadn't arrived yet, but she couldn't think of a single one.

"I'm heading home." Jed's voice startled her. "Can you lock up on your way out?"

She nodded.

"You sure?"

"Of course, go ahead. I know you said a fish is calling your name this afternoon." She motioned toward the door with a grin. At least she hoped it came across as a grin. "Be gone already."

The bell above the diner door jangled. Her smile froze as Luke shoved the door open. Her palms turned clammy.

Jed snickered and smacked Luke on the back. "Good to see ya. She's been as nervous as a frog in a cooking pot." She wanted to smack the smirk from his face.

The cowboy's head swung in her direction.

Ellie swallowed and said, "I'll be ready in a second." She sent a scowl Jed's way before she bustled into the kitchen. Her fingers shook as she rinsed the rag and laid it across the handle of the water pump. She scooped up her knitting basket, slung it over her arm, and then ran a hand over her hair.

It doesn't matter how you look, girl. Either he's upset with you or he isn't. Might as well face him.

When she reached the dining area, Luke and Jed had disappeared. She breathed a little easier when she spotted the two men talking by Luke's wagon. Ellie slipped the key out of her pocket, secured the door, and walked over to the men.

Jed waved and strolled away, a fishing pole over one shoulder and a bucket of worms in the other hand. She shivered. At least he had kept the bait outside all morning.

Luke swung her onto the seat with a thunk. A cry burst from her mouth. Not a good sign for how the afternoon would go.

He flicked the reins and the horses jolted to a start. Ellie racked her brain trying to come up with something to say. Anything.

Silence blistered between them. Within ten minutes they had reached the outskirts of his ranch. Instead of heading toward the bunkhouse, he urged the horses a different direction. Panic flew through Ellie. What exactly did he have in mind?

Just how angry was he? She swallowed hard. Should she apologize for yesterday? But how could she without drudging up Mae's past? Her twin had been gun-shy of men ever since the fella on the train ride who had stalked her on their way west. The man had refused to take no for an answer. They hadn't gotten rid of him until a federal marshal had boarded the train, and the crazed man jumped while the locomotive was in motion.

Ellie shook her head. She still couldn't believe Mae had put herself in a position to be around a man yesterday. But then they'd been protective of each other ever since they were toddlers.

Visions of the dime novels Mae read zoomed through her brain as the wagon wheels stirred up dust. People murdered and hidden where nobody would find them. Surely Luke had no such plans for her...did he?

Ellie didn't know how much time had passed while they continued across his land. She searched for his men, but didn't see any of them. A meandering stream curled its way through the brush. He stopped the wagon beside it. Mesquite trees lined the shore, and a huge boulder sat beneath one.

The horses started to shift forward. "Whoa." Luke pulled back on the reins. He secured the brake and leapt to the ground. Ellie didn't know whether to stay on the seat or try to jump down on her own. Would they be here long?

"Luke?"

Before she could make up her mind, he came around to her side and reached for her. His fingers lingered on her waist as he set her on the ground. Or had she imagined it?

"I plan to speak my mind before you start working today." He lifted the Stetson from his brow and wiped his forehead. He swung his hand in the direction of the huge rock.

They picked their way across the short distance. She lifted her skirt so it wouldn't get snagged on the cactus plants. Moisture beaded on her brow.

She rested on the edge of the boulder while he paced in front of her.

A muscle flickered in his jaw. "I don't cotton well with being lied to."

"But I..."

He held up a hand to halt her conversation. "Just hear me out."

She nodded. A tear pricked at the corner of her right eye.

"A few years back, I was engaged."

Air sucked in through her mouth before she clenched her lips tight, silencing the noise.

"My pa warned me that the gal was no good. That she didn't really care about me. Only cared about my money, and the fact I'd one day inherit this ranch." He didn't meet her eyes.

"I didn't believe him. We had words. Words I regret I didn't get a chance to take back before he died. I left in a huff, and it turned out he was right." He kicked at the dirt. "I determined never to get fooled by a woman again."

Pain washed through her. Mae should've never taken her place, or her twin should've at least told him the truth. Ellie refused to throw her sister under the wagon wheels by sharing Mae's painful past or that it was her idea to fill in. She couldn't betray her. Best if Ellie said nothing. Her jaw clenched. Why did it matter?

"Yesterday I made things right with God, asked for his forgiveness. I'm ready to see what he has for me and then—"

"You found out about Mae taking my place." She couldn't mention that her achy body had swayed her twin's decision. One didn't discuss body parts with the opposite gender. Ellie's cheeks flamed at the thought.

She closed her eyes as their betrayal sank in. While it had seemed innocent at the time and had been her sister's idea, she should have realized the hurt it could cause. Why had she never considered that in all the times they had impersonated each other? Probably because none of those times had involved a handsome young man. It didn't matter that Mae had done it without her knowledge.

Could his reaction mean he had feelings for her or was starting to? Did she want him to? She stood and moved beside him. A tremor ran through her body as she rested her fingers on

73

his forearm. The muscles tightened beneath her hand.

***

Luke studied the beautiful woman a hair's breadth away. Her touch burned through him. *Lord, help me.*

"I determined ever since my fiancée ran off to stick to bachelorhood." He swallowed. "Now I'm not so sure."

Her eyes widened and color tinged her cheeks. "Y-you're not?"

He ignored her question. "But I can't abide by someone who can't be honest." He waited for her to say something. To give some reason for the deception. But she didn't.

"I expect you won't want me to cook for you after this." She bowed her head.

"What gave you a fool notion like that?"

Her gaze shot to his, her eyes spitting nails. Surely she'd say something.

Instead she crossed her arms and hitched her chin up a notch.

So be it, he could be just as ornery. He slapped on his Stetson and strode toward the wagon without a backward glance. With a vault to the wagon seat, he released the brake and smacked the reins across the horse's back.

Who needed a woman anyway?

He could only imagine what his ma would think, leaving a lady standing in the middle of a pasture, but he refused to listen this time. Maybe walking back to the bunkhouse would give her time to get over her stubbornness. He hoped supper would be long in coming, because right now he couldn't stomach the sight of her.

The time it took to reach the barn wasn't nearly enough. *Lord, is it too much to ask that nobody be here for once?*

"Howdy, boss." Bart appeared at the door and lifted a hand. "Say, where's Ellie?"

Luke mumbled under his breath.

"What's that?" His foreman cupped his ear and came closer.

"Take care of the horses, will you?" Luke didn't wait for a response, but lengthened his stride through the barn.

It took mere minutes for him to saddle his mare and head out the opposite door of the building before his foreman could complete the task and see him out.

He spent the next several hours going over part of the herd to make sure they all were faring well. The mamas weren't too keen about him coming close to their babies. He barely missed being kicked twice. His foot still throbbed in the stirrup, from one of the run-ins when the mama had tramped on it.

He groaned inwardly when Slim rode up, a grin spread over the cowpoke's face.

"Hey, boss, I came to fetch you for chow." He brought his horse alongside Luke's. "Guess you lost track of the time."

Luke grunted.

"Me and the boys got finished with checking the fence in the other pasture a couple hours ago." His chest puffed out. "Got to spend time with Miss Ellie."

"I'll be there in a bit."

"Better come now. Miss Ellie's made my favorite, chocolate cake. You won't want to miss it."

"I said I'll be there when I can."

"Suit yourself. Just don't complain if'n it's gone when you get there." Slim waggled his eyebrows.

Luke shook his head.

"She even promised I could take her home this evening." Slim held his hands up as if in a cheer.

"She what?"

"You don't have any claim on her, do ya, boss?"

Obviously not.

Slim turned his mount. "I'll take that as a no. Thanks."

Fire roared through Luke's body. He'd do them all a favor and stay put for the next hour.

Except Slim had no sooner disappeared when another rider came into view. Luke rolled his eyes. Where could a man go for a little peace and quiet? Apparently nowhere on his ranch.

Bart brought his horse within two paces of his. He didn't say a word. Just stared at him.

Luke met his foreman's glare. Now what?

Bart shook his head. "Your ma would be disappointed in you."

"Shouldn't you be eating supper?" Luke shifted his horse back toward the herd.

"Shouldn't you be as well, instead of making that pretty gal cry?"

Luke's head swung up. Ellie was crying?

"Don't know what transpired between you two, but she looks like she lost her best friend."

"But Slim said..."

"You know Slim. He thinks all the gals are interested in him. Any fool can see she only has eyes for you."

Luke frowned. "He said he's taking her home tonight."

"What else do you expect her to do when you run off and leave the gal stranded? What's the matter with you, boss? I know your ma taught you better than that."

He squirmed like he had as a young boy when Ma'd been disappointed in him. Luke exhaled a sigh. He didn't cotton to Bart's disapproval either.

"What happened yesterday?"

"What do you mean?"

"I mean you've been stewing since supper last night." Bart quirked an eyebrow.

"They tried to pull a fast one on me." Luke shifted in the saddle.

"Who did?"

"Those twins. Ellie wasn't here yesterday."

"She wasn't? Then who was?" Bart lifted his Stetson and scratched his balding head.

"Her sister, Mae. Figured they could switch places, and I wouldn't discover their lie." His chest burned as he thought about it.

"Did you ever think that maybe they swapped places on account of Ellie not feeling up to coming? Who knows? Maybe it weren't even Ellie's idea."

"Hmm?"

"Don't you remember the first time a horse threw ya, boy? I remember it hurts something fierce the next day."

A memory rushed through him. He'd been a mere lad when he'd first been thrown. The next day, he could hardly get out of bed. Ma'd taken pity on him and prepared a tub of hot water for him to soak in. He'd had to take it easy for a couple days. Shame washed through him.

"I say you've put that gal through quite a bit the past couple days." Bart held his gaze. "I'm guessing it's high time you make things right with her."

"You don't think they did it just to trick me?"

"How can you think such a thing? I'm sure there's a good reason behind it. Did you give her a chance to explain? That gal is the sweetest thing I've seen since yer ma, God rest her soul. If you had half a brain in yer head, you'd go and beg Ellie's forgiveness and propose before she gets away. She's the best thing to come along your way in a long time. Land's sake, sometimes I think love is wasted on you young'uns. 'Specially when yer too stupid to know it when you see it." Bart shook his head. "Thought you were smarter than that, Luke."

Chapter Seven

Ellie dried the last dish and placed it in the cupboard in the bunkhouse kitchen. Luke hadn't come. All throughout the meal she'd expected him to make an appearance. To no avail. If he couldn't abide seeing her and refused to let her explain about yesterday, she had no reason to return. Of course she hadn't been free to say anything either. Not without revealing things about Mae. He'd have to figure out a way to feed the cowhands because she didn't plan to return.

She wiped her damp hands on her skirt. "Slim, I'm ready to go when you are."

The fellow had been hovering ever since he'd asked to see her home. "I got the wagon all ready, Miss Ellie." He hitched his elbow out, and she slipped her arm through it.

Minutes later he helped her onto the wagon seat. She studied the horizon and brushed a tear away. Still no sign of Luke.

Slim jumped onto the seat and smiled. His constant chatter filled the short trip home. Apparently the man liked to hear the sound of his own voice, because he didn't ask anything that required a response. Good thing too. Ellie didn't have the heart to muster up a conversation.

Why am I so bothered with a man I met mere days ago? Why does it matter what he thinks of me? She didn't need to work at the ranch, so why did she feel miserable about the notion of quitting?

She startled when Slim halted his constant chatter and looked at her expectantly.

Her cheeks warmed. "I'm sorry, what did you say?"

"I asked if I could see you home again tomorrow." He stopped the wagon in front of her home.

"I won't be returning to the ranch."

"You won't?" He scratched his head. "How come?"

"I think it's best. In fact, could you please let Luke, I mean Mr. Rogers, know I won't be able to continue?" She swung her leg over the wheel and stepped down before he could assist her. Once on the ground, she reached for her basket on the floor of the wagon.

"Is it somethin' I said, miss?"

"No, you've been a wonderful escort. Thank you." She didn't look back as she headed toward the steps of Mrs. Wright's boardinghouse and slipped inside before he could respond to her.

She no sooner had proceeded halfway up the staircase when someone pounded on the front door. With a shrug, she hurried up the rest of the steps. Whoever that was, she had no desire for more conversation. She'd almost made it to the safety of her bedroom when Mrs. Wright called out.

"EllieMae, that handsome cowboy is asking for you." The woman's voice could wake the dead.

She closed her eyes for a second and leaned against the door. Might as well get the confrontation over with. She set her belongings in the corner beside their room. A weight pressed down on her shoulders as she descended the stairs. Luke stood with his hat in his hands, his eyes piercing her.

"You two are welcome to use the sitting room." Mrs. Wright motioned. "A few of the other borders are there."

"Actually, I'd hoped we might go for a walk." Luke glanced toward the door. "That is, if you don't mind, Ellie."

Laughter rippled out from the direction of the sitting room. Maybe it would be best if she spoke with him where they wouldn't be interrupted.

"Of course."

Luke held the door open and, once outside, fumbled with his hat before placing it on his head and extending his arm to her. The tiny hairs at the back of Ellie's neck prickled.

They walked in silence for a few minutes, past the diner and dress shop. Before long they reached the edge of town, and still he hadn't spoken. The sun blazed on its final descent. A bird called to its mate.

"I owe you an apology." He pulled them to a halt and shifted, pinning her with a stare. His jaw tightened. "I should have given you a chance to explain. Bart said you were crying. I didn't mean to make you do that."

"I was peeling onions." Ellie studied the toes of her shoes, the dust lining the tips.

He gently tapped under her chin, and she swung her gaze to his. "Is that the only reason you were crying?"

She bit her lip when fresh tears sprung to her eyes. He thumbed them away, and a jolt of electricity sizzled its way through her body.

"Talk to me, Ellie."

She shook her head and hid her eyes from his scrutiny. "Mae never told me she'd fill in for me yesterday. I waited for you to come in the afternoon. In fact, I didn't find out until last night what she'd done. I..." Heat slammed into her cheeks.

"You were too sore to come?" He chucked her chin again and wiped away her tears.

She nodded. "She never intended to hurt you." She lowered her eyelashes. "Nor did I. I could barely move yesterday, and I guess Mae took pity on me even though she isn't a very good cook."

Luke snickered. "You don't say." A smile split his face. "The boys were complaining about it all last night and couldn't figure out why you made such a terrible dish when everything else has been delicious."

"Mae said..."

"Yes?"

She gathered her courage. "She said you knew she wasn't me. How? Nobody else has ever been able to tell us apart except for Ma and Pa."

"Your smile and eyes are different than hers." A muscle flickered in his cheek before he bowed his head. "I should have given you a chance to explain. I'm sorry."

Her pulse pattered in her throat. "You mentioned earlier about thinking twice about remaining a bachelor. What did you mean?"

His gaze dragged toward her face. Her lips.

"God's beginning to show me He might have other things in store for me."

"Oh." He hadn't said a word about her being a part of those things. The beating of her heart slowed to a normal pace. He hadn't meant her at all. Foolish girl. *You should have known better.*

Besides, she'd made a promise to her twin that no man would ever come between them. Especially after being carted back and forth between families who had only wanted one of them. The couple times Mae had been adopted, the new family had always ended up bringing her back to the orphanage. They'd vowed to stay together no matter what after that. No man would sway her, even if it meant living with a broken heart the rest of her life.

***

Things had been going along just fine, and then Ellie clammed up like the jaws of a steel hunting trap. Had he said something wrong? Luke shook his head. The woman's thoughts were a mystery.

He reached out and brushed a tendril of her hair behind her ear. His fingers lingered over its softness. Her eyes flew open.

She reminded him of the mare he'd gentled last spring. At first it had danced away every time he'd tried to stroke its mane. Eventually, he'd coaxed the horse to trust him. Maybe Ellie could use a little coaxing too.

He reached for her hand and held it gently in his. At first she tried to tug away but seconds later, she relaxed in his grasp. Good. He couldn't stop a grin from spreading across his face.

"I probably should head back soon. Mae will be worried about me." She turned toward town.

Not wanting to break their connection, he allowed her to lead. For now. The horse had thought it called the shots too.

"Tell me about you and your sister."

"What do you want to know?" She kept her chin forward, her body tense.

"How did you end up in Texas? I can tell from your accent you aren't a native." He squeezed her hand a trifle.

"We came in on the Orphan Train."

"Really? I never knew it came this far. From New York, right?"

She nodded.

"I read an article in the newspaper about it a few years back. How old were you?"

"Eighteen."

"Whew." He whistled. "That's pretty old to be looking for a family. Did you ever find one?"

"No, but we had plenty of marriage proposals along the way."

His gut clenched.

"How old were you when you were orphaned?"

"Ten."

"I'm sorry, Ellie." He tugged her to a halt.

She shrugged. "It was a long time ago."

"I imagine you still miss your folks though. Did you have any other siblings?"

"No. Do you?"

"Only child. Always wondered what it would be like to have a brother though. I imagine you and your sister got in a heap of trouble through the years. Especially if you swapped places with each other."

Her cheeks turned rosy, and she tugged her hand from his grasp.

He snagged it again. "Now don't get all prickly on me. I didn't mean no harm."

Her gaze shot to his before dropping to their clasped hands.

"What made you decide to stay in Texas instead of heading back to New York?"

"We liked the wide-open spaces. The city is so suffocating. When I saw this place, I told Mae I couldn't go back to life in the city again. Besides, there was nothing for us there. We were too old to be in the program any longer so we decided to get jobs here. I do miss seeing snow."

Had they no interest in marriage? "So you've been here for how many years?"

Color tinged her neck. Why didn't women ever want it known how old they were?

"Seven years."

She said the words so quietly he had to lean closer to catch them. As he did, a whiff of flowers and baked bread washed across his senses. Twenty-five. Only two years younger than he.

She licked her lips. "I told Slim..."

Why did she have to do a fool thing like bringing up his cowhand?

He tucked her closer to him, enjoying the nearness. Maybe she'd start thinking of him instead of his employee if he did something out of the ordinary. But what?

***

It took all of her will-power not to lean against Luke's side as they strolled through town. Twilight had descended. Would it be wrong to enjoy his proximity, just this once?

She cleared her throat. "I told Slim I won't be coming to work anymore."

The muscles in his arm tightened. "Why?"

"I thought it might be best."

"Aren't we past that?"

She couldn't return.

"You never did tell me exactly why you were crying this evening. And don't give me the peeling onions story."

"I, uh..." She swallowed. How could she tell him she'd cried because she wanted what she couldn't have? *Him*. Even though he'd treated her poorly earlier, she wanted him to care about her. Oh, what a mess.

"I think it's best if you show me home."

He didn't say a word as they again passed the places where she and Mae worked. Her heart broke as they drew close to her doorstop. She didn't know if she had it in her to say good-bye and walk away.

It would be for the best though. The longer she worked for Luke, the more her feelings would develop. Feelings that were best forgotten. Especially if she planned to keep her promise to Mae.

Mama used to say, *don't get close to the fire unless you plan to get burned.*

Starting tomorrow, she'd not go anywhere near the man. Not even if her life depended upon it.

Luke cleared his throat.

How long had they been standing before the front door?

"I said some things today I hope you will forgive me for." He snagged his Stetson and tucked it under one arm as he drew her closer with the other. They stood nose to nose.

"I'll see you tomorrow, Ellie, and I'll not take no for an answer." He dipped his head, and his lips met hers.

Her pulse rocketed, and her limbs had a mind of their own. Her arm wrapped around his waist and tugged him closer, while one hand explored the hair on his head. He deepened the kiss, and for a moment she was caught up in his embrace, before she broke free.

"I'm sorry. We can't." Heat flooded her face as she fumbled with the door's latch. "Good-bye, Luke."

Chapter Eight

Ellie stumbled up the stairs. She leaned her head against the doorjamb, gathering strength before facing her twin. The door swung wide.

"There you are. I've been worried something fierce. You should've been home over an hour ago. Are you hurt?" Mae drew her into the room and held her at arm's length, studying Ellie's frame. "You don't appear to be injured."

She swallowed the longing that rose up. This was where she belonged. With Mae.

"Your cheeks are flushed. What have you been doing?"

Fire blazed in Ellie's face as Luke's kiss zinged through her mind. She didn't dare tell her twin. "I, uh, went for a walk."

Her twin's brows puckered up. "You went for a walk after Luke dropped you off?"

"Luke didn't bring me home. Slim did."

Mae's eyes narrowed. "Why Slim? Did something happen? Was Luke angry about me taking your place?"

Weariness tugged at Ellie's frame. "There's nothing to worry about. I won't be working there any longer."

"He fired you." Her anger quickly dissipated as she paced their room. Her face paled. "It's my fault. Do I need to go and apologize for my deception?"

"It has nothing to do with that." Ellie turned her back on her sister and sat down to remove her high-topped shoes.

"He did something to you. I can tell."

If only her sister would give up her role as hound dog. But she had a hard time leaving things go when she got a bee in her bonnet.

Mae tugged Ellie's arm until she turned. Her twin studied Ellie's face. She refused to squirm under her sister's perusal.

"You were walking with Luke, weren't you?"

She nodded, not trusting her voice. With a tug, she tried to shift away, but her twin's grip tightened.

Mae's eyes widened. "He kissed you."

"Why would you think that?" She broke free.

"He did. How could you?"

"I didn't. He initiated it." But she hadn't complained about it, either.

"What were you thinking?"

Ellie sighed. "It was just a kiss, nothing more. I told him I won't be back, so there's nothing to worry about. I plan to keep our promise." *Even if it breaks my heart.*

"You've never been kissed before." Mae's finger circled her lips. "I haven't either, although I've thought about what it would be like."

"You have?"

Her twin nodded. "Oh, I know we promised we'd never be separated, but still, I couldn't help but think about it. Ma and Pa loved each other. I remember how they would snuggle together on the settee after we went to bed."

Ellie shook her head. "I never knew that."

Mae had a faraway look in her eyes. "I snuck out of bed a few times and found them curled up together. Ma would giggle about something Pa said, and then he'd kiss her."

"Have you ever thought about marriage?"

Mae smiled. "I have, even though we've made our pact. But I haven't found anyone worthy of changing my mind on the matter, so until then we stick together."

Ellie nodded as tears clouded her vision. Since when had Mae considered breaking their promise?

"What was it like?" Mae asked.

Maybe if she ignored her twin she'd give up on the inquisition.

"Luke's kiss? Did you enjoy it?"

The feeling of his lips pressed to hers soared in her mind. "Yes." The word came out breathlessly.

"You can't be falling for him. You've only known him for four days."

In love? Ellie shrugged. If he kept bestowing kisses on her like that, she could easily fall for him. It was why she had to stay away.

***

"Never thought I'd see the day you were pining after a fella." Jed wiped his hands on his apron.

"I am not." Ellie avoided her boss's stare. It had been two weeks since that kiss, but it still lingered in her mind.

"You can argue all you want, but you can't deny the truth shining from your eyes. Been like that ever since you quit working out there.

When are you going to take pity on the boy and speak to him?" He stacked a bunch of dirty plates beside her wash pan. "He's been showing up here every day we're open."

And on the off days, he showed up at Mrs. Wright's.

"You act like a lovesick calf. It's about time you admit you have feelings for him."

She definitely had feelings for him. No matter how hard she tried to get away from them, they kept popping up when least expected. And those longings were coming more and more frequently.

"Don't start, please." Ellie didn't have the energy to argue with her boss. It took all she had to keep telling herself to forget Luke. So far it hadn't been working.

Jed shook his head. "Don't make a fool mistake and let that boy go. He's good for you. I reckon you worry what'll happen to your sister if you get hitched. But sometimes the good Lord has plans different than ours."

She scrubbed a sudsy hand across her face. "My relationship with my sister has nothing to do with it."

"Right. That's why you both have turned down every man in town without a second glance. Don't take a genius to figure you two must have concocted some such nonsense."

"You don't understand."

Jed held up a hand. "No, I don't know what it's like to be a twin or be orphaned. I can figure you and your sister have had some rough times through the years. But have you ever thought about Jesus being a father to the fatherless? He promises to take you up and be there for you. Maybe being an orphan was part of that plan, so you'd turn to Him."

Ellie considered his speech. Jed wasn't known for giving long ones unless something stirred his dander. "I don't blame God."

"Don't you?" His brows drew together, a tiny crease forming between them.

The oatmeal she'd eaten earlier twitched in her tummy.

"Have you asked God about Luke?"

"No," Ellie said. "I don't see a reason to. I don't plan to marry."

Jed snorted. "Girl, has God told you that, or is it the fool plan you and your sister came up with?"

Ellie's hands stilled on the plate she'd been washing.

"Promises made as children aren't always meant to carry into adulthood."

"Yes, but—"

"No buts. I suggest you do some praying about the matter. My guess is you're supposed to give the boy a chance."

"What makes you such an authority on this?" Soapsuds flew as she plunged her hands back in the water.

She scrubbed the plate, rinsed it, and set it aside to dry, all the while waiting for his answer. She saw he'd stopped wiping down the counter and was staring at nothing.

He turned his gaze to her. "I let my gal get away because I was too afraid to take a chance."

"What happened?"

"She upped and married my best friend. Said she was tired of waiting for me to muster up my nerve to ask her." Jed studied her. "I don't want to see you make the same mistake."

"How did you know she was the right one? Did God speak to you?" Ellie swirled the dishrag into a glass.

He picked up a hand towel and started drying. "Have you ever had something you wanted to do, and it kept picking away at you like a chisel until you finally did something about it?"

"I'm not sure."

"I always wanted to have my own restaurant. It didn't make no sense though, since I can't cook. But I kept feeling God prompting me to go after my dream. I love chatting with the folks each day and seeing how they're doing. To learn about old widow Lawrence's rheumatism and how many fish the Whitham brothers have caught. "

"You never have told me about how you started the restaurant business."

"This place was abandoned, and I got it for cheap. I told the Lord I only had so much to use as a down payment, and this place was even cheaper than that." Jed placed a stack of dinner plates in the cupboard. "God opened the doors along the way and provided for each step. Course there can be snags in the journey, but I believe God uses those to make us stronger."

"How does that relate to how you knew the girl was the one?"

"On account of God giving me little signs with each step I took. I just was too much of a fool to act on them. I let fear grip me."

Ellie cleaned the stack of silverware. Who knew Jed gave such fine counsel? Maybe there was a reason she hadn't been able to get Luke out of her mind since he kissed her. Since she met him, actually. Could he be part of God's plan for her life?

***

Luke paced back and forth behind the diner. Every day Jed had said Ellie wasn't available. In fact, the man had even barred him from going into the kitchen to speak with her. Mrs. Wright hadn't been helpful either when he tried to catch Ellie at the boardinghouse.

He figured she escaped through the back door after her shift at the diner each day, so she could avoid him. Well, he refused to be ignored any longer. He hadn't been able to forget her. Nor did he want to.

A half hour passed, and still she hadn't shown. Perhaps he had missed her. Had she slipped out the front door after all?

The hinge screeched as the door moved outward. He held his breath. *Ellie.*

Her eyes flew open when she spotted him, and she glanced toward the diner as if seeking an escape. Not this time. He moved to stand beside her. "I've been trying to see you."

She gulped like a fish out of water. Her eyes darted back and forth. "I need to get home."

"Then I'll see you there." He held out his arm.

She hesitated for a moment before she took it. Hope surged through him.

Now that he had her beside him, he completely forgot his rehearsed speech.

She kicked a weed tuft. "Do you believe God cares about the details of our life?"

Her words surprised him. He nodded. "Most definitely. I seek Him in all I do."

"Does He answer you?" Her gaze swung to his.

He nodded. "Not always how I'd like, and sometimes the answer is long in coming. Sometimes the answer is no or wait, but He always answers me."

She nibbled on her lip. "The leaders at the Children's Aid Society said God loves us and has a plan for our lives."

He waited for her to continue.

"I asked Jesus into my heart before Ma and Pa died. But then I felt He abandoned us when we were orphaned. Nobody wanted two girls. The boys were usually the ones adopted, more so because they were stronger." She stared at her feet.

Should he say something?

"Twice Mae got adopted and I didn't. She stopped eating, and I threw fits continually at the orphanage until they returned her. I missed her something fierce. Each time her adoptive family brought her back.

"We've had a special bond all our lives. Ma used to say it's part of being a twin. I don't know if that's true or not. We just determined we would stay together no matter what."

Luke prayed for wisdom. He could never understand what it had been like for Ellie and Mae, but he didn't want to be flippant. "Sometimes pledges made in childhood aren't necessary in adulthood."

"Jed said the same thing." She studied his face for a second. "How would I know?"

"Pray about it. God will provide the solution."

"Suppose I don't like His answer."

He rubbed the back of his neck. "You still need to obey."

They had reached the boardinghouse, and he had yet to tell her how he felt about her.

Ellie paused and looked up at him, a smile teasing her lips. "Thank you for walking me home."

He couldn't resist lightly touching her face. "I'll be praying for you, Ellie that you hear clearly the answer He has for you and follow His leading." He touched his lips to hers, lingering for a moment in their sweetness. He cleared his throat and said, "I pray the answer is me."

Chapter Nine

Another week passed and still no word from Ellie. Luke sought the Lord night and day for her and for him. He beseeched Him again now as he sat on his horse, watching the herd. God had brought them together, and Luke didn't plan on letting her go. Unfortunately, he had no idea how to share what God had showed him without scaring her off. He raked a hand through his hair and slammed his Stetson in place.

The rattling of buggy wheels stirred him from his musings. His heart constricted. Ellie. He kicked his horse into a gallop.

He yanked back on the reins and vaulted from the saddle as the buggy came to a halt. His throat went dry, and his steps faltered as he came alongside it. Disappointment washed through him, souring his gut.

The young woman stared at him. "I still can't figure out how you can tell I'm not her."

He forced a smile and helped Mae from the seat. *Because I love her, not you.*

Her eyes narrowed and she tapped the side of her chin with her finger. "You look about as miserable as my sister."

His bottom lip drooped open. How was he to respond to that?

She brushed dust from her skirt. "I think it's time we talk. Especially if you plan to marry her."

Luke couldn't stop a huge grin from spreading across his face. "You think she'll have me?"

Mae tittered. "I sure hope so because she's about to drive me mad with all her longing for you."

So she'd spoken of him. It had to be a good sign. He allowed Mae to slip her arm through his as they walked across the uneven ground in the grassy pasture behind his home.

Mae shielded her eyes from the sunshine. "She hasn't said much, but I can tell it's eating her up inside. I figured I'd better come see if you can talk some sense into her. It's evident she cares for you deeply." She studied her feet. "We made a commitment to each other a long time ago that we'd stick together."

"The pledge you made as children."

"She spoke of it?" Mae's gaze shot up to meet his.

"Sort of. She didn't go into any great detail, but I had a feeling it had something to do with you. I'm guessing about not allowing any man to come between you or something along that path." He watched a calf stroll over to its mother in the field, then butt its head against her side.

Mae's shoulders drooped. "I had always hoped." She flicked away a tear and then smiled. "It was a childish promise and one I wish to release her of. I trust you'll take good care of my sister and love her—"

He nodded. "I think I started falling in love with her when I saw her tossed from that horse. Scared a good ten years off me. I knew then I couldn't live without her. Even though we've had our share of misunderstandings, I believe God brought us together."

He surveyed his calloused hands. "My ma used to knit too. One time my kitten had gotten into her latest project and snarled it to a fine mess. Ma had to tear out rows and rows of work she'd already done. She told me that relationships were like that. Sometimes they hit snags and look like a real mess, but if we take our time to mend those stitches, we still can end up with a good-looking piece."

He turned toward her. "Ma took that matted mess and made it into a scarf for me. I wore it for many years. Always reminded me that even in our mistakes in life, God can make something beautiful out of it." Luke plucked a blade of grass and nibbled on the end.

Mae fumbled with her handbag and drew out a handkerchief. She dabbed her tears. "You have a way with words, Luke Rogers."

"I don't think I'd go that far." He smiled.

"I've been meaning to tell you...I didn't try to make problems between you two. I merely wanted to help her out, that's why I took her place that day. Things haven't been the same between you two since then, and I wanted to ask for your forgiveness for the whole shenanigan. I never told her I planned to take her place, so please don't blame her."

He patted her gloved hand. "You don't need to worry about it. Sure, I misunderstood at first, but I think we worked it out. She just got scared when I kissed her."

"Yes, she mentioned it."

Pleasure soared through him.

Mae nodded. "Of course, she sloughed it off like it didn't matter, but I could tell she was withholding her true feelings about you. She hasn't told me, but I'm sure she loves you. I think she's too proud to be the first one to come to you. I need to release her from our silly pledge too, but I wanted to first find out where you stood on the matter."

"I've been praying about us for quite some time." Luke shifted toward Mae. "I love her, and I feel God has called us to be together. I'm hoping she'll have me. I've been praying she gets the same answer from the Lord that I have, and she'll listen to it."

"I know she's spent a lot of time in prayer the past few weeks."

"I've been praying to be released from waiting so I can go to speak with her."

Mae shot him a sideways look and winked. "Well, I guess you have it now. Just give me a head start back to town, so I can speak with her first."

Luke's heart took flight like the hawk overhead.

"You might want to clean up a little bit first." Mae wrinkled her nose. "You..."

He let out a roar and twirled her around. "It won't be a dull moment having you as a sister-in-law."

Her cheeks flushed as she laughed. "Don't count your pigs before they're in the pen. You first have to woo the girl. She doesn't know it, but I've been working on her wedding dress."

Luke shook his head as she waggled her brows and gave a jaunty wave.

***

Ellie sighed and closed her Bible. *Thank You for forgiving me, Lord, for blaming You about my past. I should have known that despite being orphaned, You still had a plan for me and Mae. I couldn't see it then, and I don't know if I have all the answers now either, but I trust You to show them to me in Your timing. Thank You for Your promise to stay with me and never leave me. To never forsake me.* She glanced out the window. *Is it too much to ask for more than that, Lord?*

A heavy sigh seeped from her lips. She had received an answer to her prayers this week but had yet to receive direction on what she should do about it.

She checked the window again. Mae should have been home from work over an hour ago. She'd missed Mrs. Wright's dinner. Not that Ellie'd had much of an appetite for the chicken and biscuits the woman had prepared. Her landlady had clucked all through the meal about her lack of appetite. Fortunately, the other two boarders hadn't been present to hear the woman's constant scolding.

A warm breeze stirred the curtain, and she plunked a hat on her head and tied the ribbons under her chin. Perhaps a walk would get her in the right frame of mind. It couldn't hurt. She snuck down the steps, eager to avoid Mrs. Wright in case she came up with something new to reprimand her about.

She breathed a little easier once she'd closed the door behind her. Ellie strolled past the shops and the livery, heading out of town. She soon realized she'd traveled in the direction of Luke's ranch. Oh, how she missed him.

She studied the horizon, shielding her eyes from the sun. A buggy ambled toward her. She moved to the grass beside the dirt road to keep out of the way. Was that...yes. Her sister was driving it. How curious. Just what had she been up to?

"Mae?"

Her twin smiled. "Nice to see you out of our room for a change."

Ellie's ire rose. "I go out every single day, and you know it."

Mae shook her head. "Only to go to work. Then you slink back home again. Get in, and I'll give you a ride back."

Ellie gaped at her sister before she climbed aboard. Since when did Mae get such gumption? "If you ask me, it's silly for you to give me a ride when we're only a hundred yards from town."

"After I return the carriage, you and I need to chat."

Her stomach pitched. Uh-oh, what did her twin have in mind?

Moments later, they strolled arm-in-arm at the outskirts of town, behind the livery. Mae had said she didn't want them to be interrupted, which really set Ellie's nerves on edge.

"Spit it out. The suspense is killing me. What's going on?"

Mae plucked a flower and took her time in responding. "You, my dear, have been denying yourself for far too long."

"W-what do you mean?" Her pulse raced.

"Denying yourself the things in life you really want. Or should I say *the person* you really want." A twinkle flashed in Mae's eyes, so like hers.

Could she mean what Ellie thought she meant?

Mae sighed and stared forward for a moment. Finally, she said, "I always feared the times we were separated."

A weight pressed and threatened to take Ellie's breath.

Mae fingered the bow on her straw hat. "Ma told me once that I would never understand what God had for me as long as I lived in your shadow."

"I don't remember that. I can't imagine why she thought you lived in my shadow."

Mae's eyes took on a far-away look. "You tried new things while I watched from the safety of the house." She turned to Ellie and a bittersweet smile lined her twin's face. "You were helping Pa. You always did like running about the farm with him."

"While you were usually by Ma's side. She loved that you had such a knack for sewing. I think she feared I'd never learn how to sew a button on or hem a garment, let alone make one." Ellie laughed at the memory. "What has you thinking about that?"

Mae hugged her. "It's time I release you from our pledge. I think God has different paths ahead of us for the future."

Ellie's heart lightened. "You're trying to get rid of me."

Her twin grinned. "Heavens no, but I think you are at a point where you have to follow what God is calling *you* to do. My guess is it has something to do with a handsome blond cowboy."

Her thoughts scurried like a cluster of baby chicks trying to keep up with their mama. Mae was releasing her? To be with Luke? "Are you sure?"

Mae nodded, and a tear trickled down her cheek. "You know I'll miss you terribly, but I want you to be happy, Ellie. Our promise to stay together was needed for a time...when we both were young and had to cling to the only family we had left. Ma and Pa want us to follow our own inclinations, to be free to be the people God created us to be.

"We'll always have a special bond. Being twins makes it so. But I don't ever want to stand in the way of you seeking out and searching after what God has called you to do. And when you know what it is, which I think you already do—"Mae took Ellie's hand and smiled through a sheen of tears—"then you should go for it with all you have. I won't stand in your way."

"Oh, Mae, thank you." She hauled her sister into a tight hug. "I can't wait to see what God has in store for both of us."

The sound of thundering hooves snagged Ellie's attention. If only she could view around the building to see the road.

Mae's face lit up. "I think you're about to find just what He has in store for you."

A single rider. Could it be?

Mae placed her hand on Ellie's arm. "We both know you have feelings for the man."

"Jed suggested I pray about Luke, to see if God wanted us to be together." She fingered her frayed sleeve.

"Have you?"

Ellie nodded. She strained to hear if the horse had ridden past, not wanting to appear too obvious.

"What has God shown you?" Mae's brows rose.

She snuck a glance in the direction of the road but didn't see anyone. It must have been someone other than Luke riding into town. Surely other people lived in his direction. Silly girl. With a sigh, she turned her attention back to her sister.

"I asked God to forgive me for blaming Him about Pa and Ma. I committed to following after Him no matter what." Ellie grinned at her twin. "Then I asked God to soften your heart about our promise and not to be upset with me when I told you I can't keep it any longer."

"Why is that?" Merriment shone from her sister's face.

She licked her lips and said, "Because I love Luke Rogers, and I believe He is what God has for me. Now I have to figure out how to tell him without coming across as being too forward."

Mae snickered.

Her response wasn't quite what Ellie had expected.

"I think many things about you, my dear," a deep voice rumbled behind her back, "but being too forward isn't one of them."

She spun around to see Luke standing before her. His hair slicked back and a bouquet of wildflowers in his hands couldn't match the brightness of his smile. He came. She had the sneaking suspicion her twin had something to do with his appearance.

He moved closer to her, and the scent of musk and fresh air washed over her. He smelled like home.

Chapter Ten

Luke gathered Ellie into his arms. His eyes dipped closed for a moment, enjoying the feel of having her there. When he opened his eyes, Mae had disappeared. Smart girl. He smiled.

Ellie sighed and nestled closer. Could she hear the bucking of his heart?

"Is it true?" He nuzzled his lips against her hair, inhaling the scent of baked bread.

"Hmm. What's that?" Color tinged her cheeks.

"You said you love me."

Her face turned a darker shade of red. "You're the one who's supposed to declare it first. I didn't intend for you to hear—"

"You don't care for me?" His breathing came in sharp bursts. Perhaps he'd heard her wrong.

"No, I mean, of course I do." She stepped from his grasp and wrapped her arms around her waist.

The steel bands around his lungs loosened, and he drew her back into his embrace. "I love you Ellie Stafford, and I want to make you my wife as soon as possible."

She tilted her head back and studied him. "You sure you don't just care about having a cook for you and your men?"

His gaze dropped to her lips. "Cooking is far from my mind. Besides, I already hired a new cowpoke who can handle feeding the fellas."

"I hadn't heard that."

He took a step back, but kept his fingers laced through hers. "Yep."

"Then there is no need for me."

"Girl, don't you ever think that. I have need of you." He dropped to one knee. "Will you marry me, Ellie? I've been praying and know God wants us to be together. You satisfy me in a way no other woman has—"

"Not even what's-her-name, the woman you were engaged to?" A tear escaped her eye and ran down her cheek.

Luke prayed it was a tear of joy.

He stood and grazed his finger across her lips. "You don't ever have to worry, little filly. She could never compare with you. I didn't understand the love between a man and a woman until I got to know you."

"You're sure—?"

In answer he dipped his head and claimed her lips.

***

Time stood still as Luke kissed her. The thudding of her heart filled her ears...or could it be his heart she was hearing? At some point she became aware of their surroundings and the fact that anybody could happen by at a given moment. She had no idea how much time had passed. With a sigh, she broke the connection between their lips.

"Yes, I'll marry you, Luke Rogers."

He let out a whoop and swung her around, her legs flailing beneath her long skirt.

She giggled. "Put me down."

"You've made me the happiest man in all Calder Springs." His face beamed.

"I don't know about that." She couldn't help teasing. "I heard the Millers had their baby this morning."

"I can shout our news for all to hear. Perhaps that will convince you." His eyes twinkled.

She laid a finger over his mouth. "Don't you dare."

He waggled his eyebrows. "Better not dare me. I've been known to follow through with any dare I've been given."

Joy surged through her. It would be interesting getting to learn more and more about this man she loved with all her heart.

"I hope you don't mind if I keep knitting garments for the orphans in New York." She nibbled on her lower lip. "I'd like to be able to continue to do something for the children there even though I haven't gotten much knitting accomplished lately."

He ran his fingers along the side of her face before cupping her cheek. A ripple ran through her at his touch. "Darling, I want you to do what will make you happy and what you feel God has called you to do. As long as I'm part of that equation.

"Ma knitted too. I told Mae about it earlier. I'd like for us to cast on stitches together as we work to build a new relationship as one." He dropped a kiss on her temple.

"I never knew you had such a way with words."

"There's a lot for you to learn about me, darling." He nuzzled her neck. "I think I understand why knitting those things means so much to you. You remember what it was like to be an orphan." He dropped a peck on her lips. "I can't imagine what you went through without your parents. I'm thankful that even though you were orphaned, God still provided for you."

She peered at Luke. Love shone through his eyes. "I guess we are both orphans now, aren't we?"

He blinked a few times before answering her. "I never thought about it before, but I suppose we are. Although I like to think that we both have a heavenly Father who loves us in a way like no other love we've ever experienced."

"I like that." Ellie's eyes misted.

"Other than being my wife"—he tugged her closer—"is there anything else you've always wanted to do?"

She ran her teeth across her lips. Did she dare tell him?

He searched her face.

"Promise me you won't laugh."

"Tell me, Ellie."

"I've always wanted to study medicine. Oh, I know I can't ever go to a fancy medicine school, nor do I think I want to anymore." She smiled at him. "When I was with my pa on the farm, I wanted to know how to make folks and critters better. It probably sounds silly." She dipped her head, afraid to meet his gaze.

He tapped her chin, and she glanced at him. "Darling, it doesn't sound silly at all. Besides, my ma always said continually seeking out knowledge and learning is a good thing. In fact, I think having that kind of knowledge is important, especially on the ranch with the cowpokes and for the future, when we have children. "

Heat flooded her face at the thought of little ones running around the ranch. Little boys with curly blond hair and bright blue eyes.

***

Five Days Later
Ellie fingered the shimmery ivory material, the fabric rustling as it slipped through her hands. She tweaked her pale cheeks and studied her reflection one last time before turning to her sister. "I hope Luke will be pleased."

Her twin settled a tulle waist-length veil over Ellie's carefully pinned hair, securing it with a hairpin. Mae flounced the material until she had it sitting just so.

"There, you look gorgeous. Of course Luke will be pleased. Besides, more than likely, the big lunk won't even notice your dress. He'll only have eyes for you."

"You never did tell me how you managed to create such a beautiful dress in less than a week." Ellie couldn't help touching the fabric again.

Her twin laughed. "I've been working on it for several weeks."

"But I wasn't even engaged yet."

"I figured you would be. Mrs. Beadle allowed me to sew on it when we had a lull in orders." Mae pulled her into a brief hug. "I'm going to miss you so."

"Are you sure you don't want me to—?"

"Don't be silly. Of course you're going to marry the man and not think twice about me. I'll be fine. It's high time I discover what God has for me too."

"It's not like I'll be living far away. Only a little over a mile or so." Tears pricked Ellie's eyes. "You'll visit me often, won't you?"

"You'll be a newlywed and won't want your twin getting in the way."

"You'll never be in the way. Luke and I want you to come as often as you want. We've talked about it already."

"We can discuss it later. We better get downstairs."

Ellie tugged her sister back for another hug. "We both love you. I'll be praying God brings someone special into your life too."

"I don't know about that." Mae shook her head. "I don't have any intention on getting married."

Ellie scrutinized her twin. "I still plan to pray about it for you and have already."

A knock thudded against their bedroom door. Mrs. Wright poked her head around the door before pushing it open all the way. "You two should be finished with all the primping. I think the bridegroom is going to pace a hole in my parlor floor if you don't get down there straight away."

"Yes, ma'am." Ellie took a deep breath.

Mrs. Wright handed her a bouquet of flowers. "I know you don't have any folks, but I wanted you to know, dear, how much I've come to love you and..." She glanced back and forth between the two of them. "Oh, I'll never be able to tell you two apart." She kissed both of their cheeks. "Hurry down, and I'll start playing the piano."

Without a backward glance, the woman scurried out of the room and down the flight of stairs.

"Well, here goes." Ellie twined her arm through her sister's and together they walked down the steps.

When they reached the bottom, the music swelled. The doors to the parlor were flung open, and chairs lined the small room. Jed, Bart, Slim, and the other cowpokes grinned at her. She hardly recognized them as she got closer. They were all spruced up and smelling their best.

Her gaze caught Luke's at the front of the room. He stood beside the minister. A huge smile plastered across his face. Her heart skipped a beat. He wore a dark suit and a string tie, his blond curls tamed for the moment.

Mae hugged her and took her place beside her once they reached the front of the room. Bart stood beside Luke.

Ellie's heart quickened as the minister said, "Dearly beloved."

The ceremony flew by on wings like a hummingbird and soon she heard the minister say, "You may now kiss your bride."

Luke lifted her veil and ran a finger along her cheek, sending shivers up her spine before he touched his lips to hers, claiming her as his own.

"I love you, Ellie Rogers," he whispered in her ear before planting another kiss on her lips.

Hoots and whistles sounded from his men. "Way to go, boss."

Her laughter bubbled over and broke free. "It definitely won't be dull at the ranch, will it?"

Luke laughed. "It's been a while since they've had a woman living there, but they'll love and protect you now that you are one of the bunch."

Mrs. Wright scurried to the piano and belted out a lively tune as they walked the short aisle.

Luke stole another kiss before the music stopped and her landlady bustled toward them. "Enough of the kissing. Let's eat."

Mae followed in the older woman's wake, giving them both a hug. Tears streaked her cheeks. "I couldn't be any happier for both of you." She whipped out a handkerchief and dabbed her eyes.

A knock sounded at the front door, and Mrs. Wright waddled over to answer it. "Now who could that be? Don't folks know I've got a reception to tend to?"

The small group of well-wishers quieted, and all eyes swung toward the door as a man with a little girl in his arms stepped into the room. "I'm so sorry. I hadn't realized there was a party going on today. I'll come back later."

The wee sprite lifted her head from the man's shoulder and said, "Look, Papa, a wedding. Isn't her dress be-uu-tiful?"

"Yes, dear." He kissed his daughter on her little brown-haired head and dipped his hat. "Again, I apologize for the intrusion."

He slipped away and closed the door behind them.

"I wonder who they are," Jed said. "I've never seen them before."

Ellie darted a glance at her sister. Mae's eyes still studied the spot where the man and his daughter had been. *Interesting*. Maybe her twin would open her heart to love one day too.

"Let's eat," Mrs. Wright called from the dining room.

"Go on ahead, everyone." Luke motioned to their friends and Mae. "I want a minute with my wife first."

Once they were alone, Luke pressed a wrapped package into her hands. "I have this for you."

"But Luke, I don't have a gift for you."

He kissed the tip of her nose. "It's not exactly a wedding gift. Open it."

She untied the twine and folded back the paper. A ball of yarn bounced to the floor. Luke bent down and scooped it up. Two knitting needles and a book poked out of the package. When she flipped the book over, she read the title.

"How did you happen to get a medical book?"

"Turns out my new cowpoke and cook had a brother who studied at the medical school in Galveston but died before he could finish. Anyway, my new hired man gave the book to me. I thought you might be interested in it."

Pleasure soared through Ellie. Luke understood her, accepted her, and championed her dreams. She sniffed and wiped away a tear. "And the yarn and needles?"

His cheeks flushed. "That's to let my little filly know our hearts are knit together as one."

He took her in his arms and branded her with his kiss.

Note from the author:

The Twins & Needles series continues in November 2016, with Mae's story.

Love in the Seams

31482010R00085

Made in the USA
Middletown, DE
01 May 2016